little
Miss
Helpful

by Roger Hargreaves

Little Miss Helpful was one of those people who love to help other people, but who end up helping nobody.

Do you know what I mean?

I mean, for instance, like the time when one of Mr Tall's shoelaces came undone.

Now, if you're as tall as Mr Tall, tying your shoelaces isn't the easiest thing in the world.

As you can imagine!

"Let me help!" cried Little Miss Helpful rushing up.

Then, somehow, she managed to tie Mr Tall's shoelaces together.

And he fell over!

And, if you're as tall as Mr Tall, falling over hurts.

BANG!

"Ouch!" he said, rubbing his head.

"Let me help!" cried Little Miss Helpful, and rushed off to get some sticking plaster.

And rushed back and stuck it on Mr Tall.

Over his mouth!

"Mmmm mm mmm!" he said.

He was trying to say "Take it off!"

But that's rather difficult to do with sticking plaster stuck over your mouth.

Little Miss Helpful looked at him with concern.

"Let me help!" she cried.

And ripped the sticking plaster off his mouth.

"Owwwwwwwwwwwwwwwwwwwch!" he cried.

"That hurt!"

"Would you like me to get some cream for your sore mouth?" she asked anxiously.

"No!" he groaned. "Go away!"

Now do you know what I mean about people like Little Miss Helpful who help nobody?

Last year, in April I think it was, Mr Happy woke up feeling not very well.

The doctor had to be called, and he came to Mr Happy's house, which is on a hill, by a lake.

"Oh dear," said the doctor when he saw
Mr Happy.

"Measles!"

Mr Happy's face fell.

"Now you're to stay tucked up nice and warm
in bed, and get lots of rest, and take this
medicine three times a day," said the doctor.

And went!

Mr Happy settled down to sleep.

He'd just fallen asleep when there was a loud knock at his front door.

"Oh dear," groaned Mr Happy, and staggered off to open it.

You can guess who it was.

Can't you?

"I've come to help," she cried.

"But..." protested Mr Happy.

"But nothing!" cried Little Miss Helpful.

"Now off to bed with you while I get on with everything!"

She looked around.

"This place needs a good clean," she said.

Mr Happy had just dropped off to sleep again when Miss Helpful poked her head around his bedroom door.

"Have you got a scrubbing brush?" she asked.

Poor Mr Happy had to get up and show her where it was.

And then he went back to bed.

To sleep!

Little Miss Helpful stepped back to admire the kitchen floor she'd just scrubbed.

And.

Trod on the soap!

And.

Fell head over heels!

And.

Got her head stuck in the bucket!

And.

Because she couldn't see where she was going, walked into a shelf full of saucepans!

Which fell all over the floor, with a terrible clatter.

And.

Because she couldn't see where she was going, Little Miss Helpful stepped in one of the saucepans and got it stuck on her foot.

And.

Because she had to hop, she fell over against the refrigerator door, which flew open and everything inside fell out!

All over Little Miss Helpful!

Poor Mr Happy awoke with a jump at the terrible commotion.

He groaned, got out of bed, went to the kitchen and opened the door.

He couldn't believe his eyes.

There, in the middle of a pile of broken eggs, and a scrubbing brush, and rolling saucepans, and a lot of water, and spilt milk, and squashed butter, and bent saucepan lids, and a piece of soap, sat Little Miss Helpful!

With a bucket on her head!!

And a saucepan on her foot!!!

"Help!" came a voice from inside the bucket.

Mr Happy seized the bucket, and pulled as hard as ever he could.

And pulled.

And pulled.

POP!

The bucket came off the top of Little Miss Helpful's head like a cork out of a bottle!

Mr Happy shot backwards like a bullet from a gun!

Crash!

He went flying through the kitchen door!

He shot across the garden, and straight through his garden hedge!

He rolled down the hilly field behind his garden!

Faster and faster!

And.

SPLASH!

He finished up in the lake.

With the bucket in his hand.

And a little figure, with a saucepan on one foot, came half running, half hopping, out of Mr Happy's house.

"Let me help!" she cried.